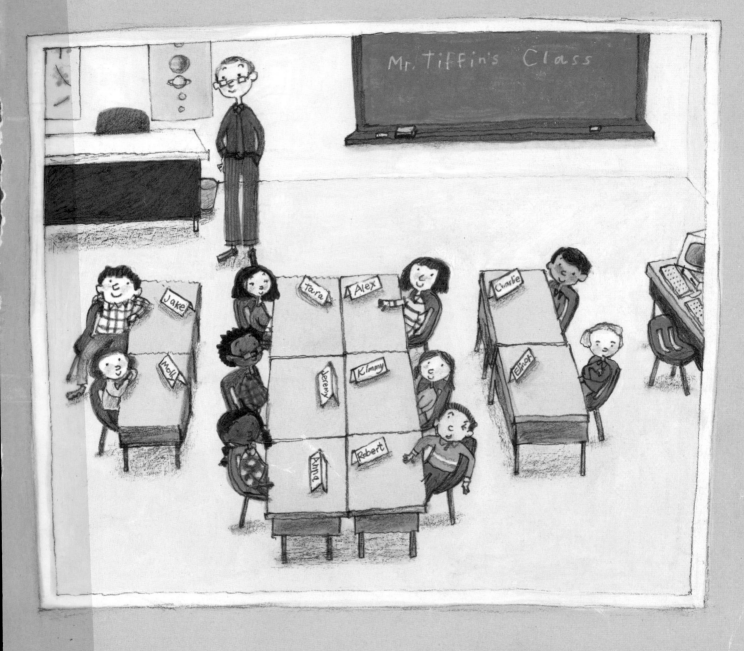

For Schwartz and Wade—M.M.
For Zachary—G.B.K.

Text copyright © 2007 by Margaret McNamara
Illustrations copyright © 2007 by G. Brian Karas

Published in the United States by Schwartz & Wade Books,
an imprint of Random House Children's Books, a division of Random House, Inc., New York.

Schwartz & Wade Books and colophon are trademarks of Random House, Inc.

www.randomhouse.com/kids

Educators and librarians, for a variety of teaching tools, visit us at
www.randomhouse.com/teachers

Library of Congress Cataloging-in-Publication Data

McNamara, Margaret.
 How Many Seeds in a Pumpkin? / Margaret McNamara ;
illustrated by G. Brian Karas. — 1st ed.
   p. cm.
 Summary: Charlie, the smallest child in his first grade class, is
amazed to discover that of the three pumpkins his teacher brings to
school, the smallest one has the most seeds.
  ISBN: 978-0-375-84014-2 (trade) ISBN: 978-0-375-94014-9 (lib. bdg.)
 [1. Size—Fiction. 2. Pumpkin—Fiction. 3. Counting—Fiction.
 4. Schools—Fiction. 5. Self-perception—Fiction.]   I. Karas, G. Brian,
ill. II. Title.
PZ7.M232518Ho 2007
[E]—dc22
2006016866

The text of this book is set in Century Schoolbook.
The illustrations are rendered in gouache, acrylic, and pencil on paper.
Book design by Rachael Cole

PRINTED IN THE UNITED STATES OF AMERICA

10 9 8 7 6 5 4 3

First Edition

The author wishes to acknowledge the Department of Horticultural Science at
North Carolina State University for its help with the pumpkin facts in this book.

how many seeds in a pumpkin?

By Margaret McNamara
Illustrated by G. Brian Karas

schwartz & wade books · new york

Charlie liked school. He liked his teacher, Mr. Tiffin. He liked his best friend, Alex. But he did not like lining up to go into school. Mr. Tiffin's class lined up by size, tallest to smallest or smallest to tallest. Charlie was the smallest in the class, every time.

One chilly fall morning, Charlie was surprised to see three bright orange pumpkins on Mr. Tiffin's desk. One pumpkin was big, one was medium, and one was small.

"How many seeds in a pumpkin?" Mr. Tiffin asked the class. "Does anybody know?

Nobody knew, but everybody had ideas.

"The biggest one has the most," said Robert. "I bet it has one million seeds." Robert was the tallest boy in the class.

"The medium one has five hundred," Elinor said. Elinor always sounded as if she knew exactly what she was talking about.

"The tiny one has twenty-two," said Anna. Anna liked even numbers better than odd ones.

1,000,000   750
500   15
22   399
137   100
900

    Mr. Tiffin wrote down all the guesses on the blackboard.
    Charlie was very quiet. "What are you thinking, Charlie?"
asked Mr. Tiffin.
    "I'm thinking that all the best guesses are taken," Charlie said.
    "Why don't we open these pumpkins up and see?" said
Mr. Tiffin.

The next day, the kids in Mr. Tiffin's class brought in spoons for scooping and bowls for holding and plastic bags for throwing out. They covered the floor with newspaper. They put on their smocks. "It's a messy business, counting pumpkin seeds," said Mr. Tiffin. But the class was ready.

After Mr. Tiffin cut a circle around each pumpkin's stem, Kimmy, Alex, and Jake pulled off the caps. The children peered inside.

"This big one definitely has the most," said Robert.

"We'll see," said Mr. Tiffin.

The pumpkin pulp was slimy and stringy, and the seeds were hard to get out.

When the children were finished, there were

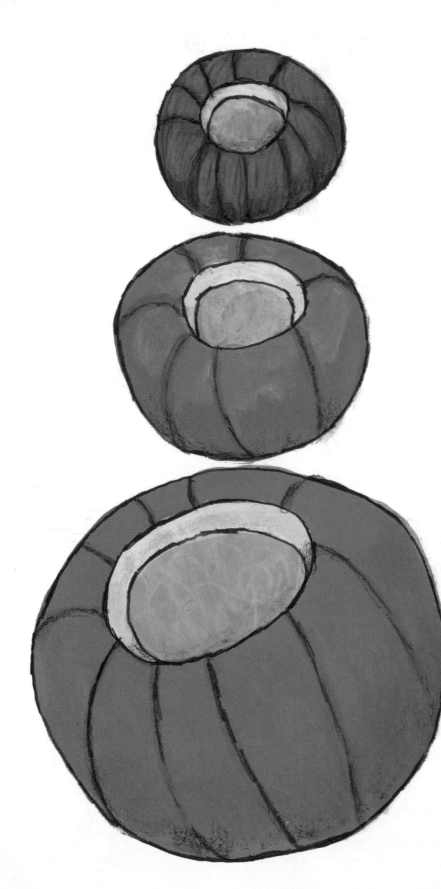

three

empty

pumpkins,

three   full   bowls,

and twenty messy hands.

"Tomorrow we will find out the answer to our
question," said Mr. Tiffin. "Tonight your homework
is to think about how we should count all the seeds."

That afternoon, Mr. Tiffin dried the seeds.

The next day, he put them in three paper bags marked Big, Medium, and Small.

"Did you do your thinking homework?" he asked the class.

"Yes," Alex said. "I think we should just guess."

"I think we should count very, very carefully," said Tara.

"I think we should count by twos, fives, and tens," said Molly.

The class agreed that Molly had a good idea.

Robert, Kimmy, and Jake all wanted to count the seeds in the big pumpkin by twos. Anna asked if she could join them. "We can be the Twos Club!" she said.

They practiced counting. "Two, four, six, eight, ten, twelve," they said together.

Jeremy, Tara, Elinor, Molly, and Alex liked counting by fives. "We'll count the seeds in the medium pumpkin," said Molly. "We can be the Fives Club."

"Five, ten, fifteen, twenty!" they cheered.

"I'll take the smallest pumpkin," said Charlie. "I guess I'll be in the Tens Club."

"Good idea," said Mr. Tiffin.

"Ten, twenty, thirty," Charlie began.

Soon there were many groups
of seeds in front of each pumpkin.

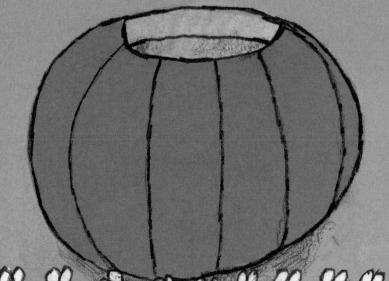

the Twos Club

"See?" said Robert. "The Twos Club has the most."
They had 170 pairs of seeds.

the Fives Club

"We have lots, too," said Elinor. They had
63 groups of 5 seeds, and one seed left over.

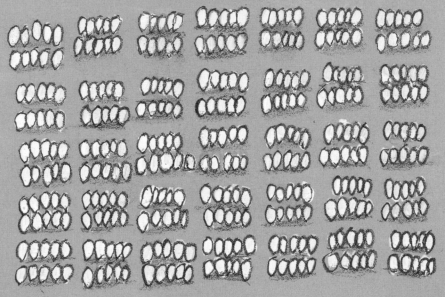

the Tens Club

Charlie had exactly 35 groups of 10 seeds.

Robert looked at the seeds in front of Charlie.
"You don't have a whole lot," he said.

"Let's get counting!" said Mr. Tiffin.

"Two, four, six, eight, ten, twelve . . . ," began Robert, Kimmy, Jake, and Anna.

It took a long time to count 170 pairs of seeds. "My brain hurts," said Anna.

The biggest pumpkin had 340 seeds. "Almost a million," said Jake.

The fives were a little easier.

"Five, ten, fifteen, twenty, twenty-five . . . ," chanted Jeremy, Tara, Elinor, and Molly.

There were 316 seeds in the medium pumpkin. "Too bad for you," said Robert.

"It's not a contest," said Molly.

The tens were the fastest of all, since there were
just 35 groups.

"Ten, twenty, thirty, forty . . . ," Charlie counted
to himself. "This can't be right," he said.

"What can't be right?" asked Mr. Tiffin.

"There are three hundred and fifty seeds in my little pumpkin," said Charlie. "That means it has the most of all."

"So it does," said Mr. Tiffin.

"Congratulations, Charlie!" said Alex.

"The Tens Club wins!"

"It's not a contest," said Robert.

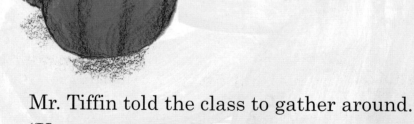

Mr. Tiffin told the class to gather around.

"You can never tell just how many seeds are in a pumpkin until you open it up," he said. "But there may be some clues. Take a good look at these."

The class did.

"Charlie's is darker orange," said Anna.

"And it has more lines on the outside," said Robert.

"Yep," said Mr. Tiffin. "For each line on the outside, there is a row of seeds on the inside."

"That's good to know," said Elinor.

"And the longer the pumpkin grows, the more lines it gets," he added. "Its skin gets darker, too."

"So even though my pumpkin was the smallest, it was on the vine the longest," said Charlie.

"Exactly," agreed Mr. Tiffin.

When it was time to go home, the class lined up by the door.

"Smallest to tallest this time," said Mr. Tiffin.
Robert was at the back. Elinor was in the middle.
Charlie was at the front.

"Small things can have a lot going on inside them," Charlie said to Mr. Tiffin.

And then they left the classroom, with Charlie leading the way.

Charlie's Pumpkin Facts

1. Pumpkin seeds are small but powerful. A whole huge pumpkin grows from a tiny seed.

2. You can eat pumpkin seeds if you want, but you should ask somebody to roast them first. They contain lots of vitamin A.

3. If you plant pumpkin seeds, do it after the ground warms up in spring. You'll need a LOT of space for them to grow. Pumpkins grow on vines.

4. It takes about four months for a pumpkin to grow to full size. So plant your seeds by June if you want a pumpkin for Halloween.

5. Is a pumpkin a vegetable? No, it's a fruit!

6. Some pumpkins are small. (I like those.) Some pumpkins are really, really big. Usually, big pumpkins don't taste very good. Small, sweet pumpkins are the kind you should use to make a pumpkin pie.

7. Counting by twos and fives and tens makes counting go faster. (That's not really a pumpkin fact, but it's true.)

Big

A Note from Mr. Tiffin

I looked pretty carefully for those three pumpkins, so that Charlie, Robert, Anna, and the other students would not be able to predict what was inside. Pollination, pumpkin variety, and time on the vine determine how many lines are on a pumpkin—and how many seeds are inside. Size alone is not the most important thing—which worked out great for Charlie.